Dear Parent:
Your child's love of reading starts here!

Every child learns to read in a different way and at his or her own speed. Some go back and forth between reading levels and read favorite books again and again. Others read through each level in order. You can help your young reader improve and become more confident by encouraging his or her own interests and abilities. From books your child reads with you to the first books he or she reads alone, there are I Can Read Books for every stage of reading:

SHARED READING
Basic language, word repetition, and whimsical illustrations, ideal for sharing with your emergent reader

BEGINNING READING
Short sentences, familiar words, and simple concepts for children eager to read on their own

READING WITH HELP
Engaging stories, longer sentences, and language play for developing readers

READING ALONE
Complex plots, challenging vocabulary, and high-interest topics for the independent reader

ADVANCED READING
Short paragraphs, chapters, and exciting themes for the perfect bridge to chapter books

I Can Read Books have introduced children to the joy of reading since 1957. Featuring award-winning authors and illustrators and a fabulous cast of beloved characters, I Can Read Books set the standard for beginning readers.

A lifetime of discovery begins with the magical words "I Can Read!"

*Visit www.icanread.com for information
on enriching your child's reading experience.*

The Berenstain Bears' Lemonade Stand Copyright © 2014 by Berenstain Publishing, Inc. Printed in the United States of America.
All Rights Reserved. No part of this book may be used or reproduced in any manner whatsoever without written permission
except in the case of brief quotations embodied in critical articles and reviews. For information address HarperCollins Children's
Books, a division of HarperCollins Publishers, 10 East 53rd Street, New York, NY 10022.
www.icanread.com

Library of Congress catalog card number: 2013950292
ISBN 978-0-06-207545-1 (trade bdg.)—ISBN 978-0-06-207544-4 (pbk.)

14 15 16 17   LP/WOR   10 9 8 7 6 5 4 3 2 1   ❖   First Edition

The Berenstain Bears'®
Lemonade Stand

Mike Berenstain

Based on the characters created by Stan and Jan Berenstain

HARPER

An Imprint of HarperCollinsPublishers

It is a hot day.

Brother, Sister, and Honey Bear
play outside.

Mama brings them lemonade.

Ahh! It is good.

Mailbear Bob comes by.

He is very hot.

"May I have some

lemonade?" he asks.

"I will give you a quarter."

Mailbear Bob drinks the lemonade.

Ahh! It is good.

"Here is your quarter," he says.

"Let's sell more lemonade,"
says Brother.

The cubs set up a lemonade stand.

They make a sign:

"Lemonade—25 cents."

Some bears are mowing
the lawn next door.
They are very hot.
They see the lemonade stand.

"We would like some lemonade," say the lawn bears.

They drink it down.

Ahh! It is good.

Their neighbor comes outside.

"I am having a party," she says.

"My guests will all want

lemonade."

Her guests arrive.

They all drink lemonade.

Ahh! It is good.

19

Some other neighbors come outside.

They want lemonade, too.

But the cubs are running out of

lemonade.

"Don't worry!" say the neighbors.

"We will help."

They bring out more drinks.
They bring out food to eat.

Some cubs come by.

"A block party!" they say.

They start to play music.

They start to dance.

It is a big party!

Farmer Ben sees the party.

He has a load of things from his farm.

He starts to sell fruit and other good things.

It is getting dark.

How will the party end?

Grizzly Gus has fireworks.

He sets them off.

They are very pretty!

The party is over.

Everyone goes home.

The cubs take down their
lemonade stand.
They go inside.
They are very tired.
They are very hot.

Mama brings them lemonade.

Ahh! It is good.

"That will be twenty-five cents,"

says Mama.

They all laugh at Mama's joke!